FBI OPEN UP!

By: Honey Beez and Ruby Gem

Copyright © 2023 Honey Beez
All rights reserved.
ISBN: 9798389117471
Photos from pixabay.com

DEDICATION

This book is dedicated to Grandpa and Daddy. Also to law enforcement thank you for protecting us.

Table of Contents:

About the Author	**4**
About the Author	**5**
FBI OPEN UP!	**6**

ABOUT THE AUTHOR

Honey is a retired computer scientist and mother. She is the author of many books.

Website: https://beedefense.net
Twitter: https://twitter.com/HoneyBeez0x

Facebook: https://www.facebook.com/honey0x

ABOUT THE AUTHOR

Ruby Gem is the daughter of Honey Beez and nickname is "sugar tornado". Ruby is age 8 and in 2nd grade. We are still practicing our writing so we take turns telling this story, for the most part.

FBI OPEN UP!

Once there was a little girl born into a hacker family…

Then they had to buy a home and brought the baby girl home and eat foodddddd an the fbi have eat the home ●

The little girl had to move away and now she lived with Mommy and family. Mommy was shocked one day when they went to a town event and at the booth for the police officers, the little girl told the officers that she wanted to be a police officer one day! Mommy was shocked!

1 day the girl was teen and she wanted to see her sis so bad that they went on a trip and the teen girl saw THE FBIIIIIIIIII so she asked the fbi R YOU MY SIS the fbi say no cus i am you car

It was funny but one day they were driving and they passed a police station and Mommy wondered what it would be like for her daughter to really be a police officer! What would her father say if he knew?!

So the teen girl named Ella saw the FBIIIIIIIIII so she said to her mmammama :Ella:mama can we go to the fbi? An say is we can sleep here an do a party an mack your home a lot more good looking

So you can imagine Mommy's continued surprise when one day her daughter watched a video on the internet that said "FBI OPEN UP!"

And then she has not stopped saying this since...

She is obsessed with the FBI!
She says "FBI OPEN UP!" to me at least once a day and everytime I jump up!

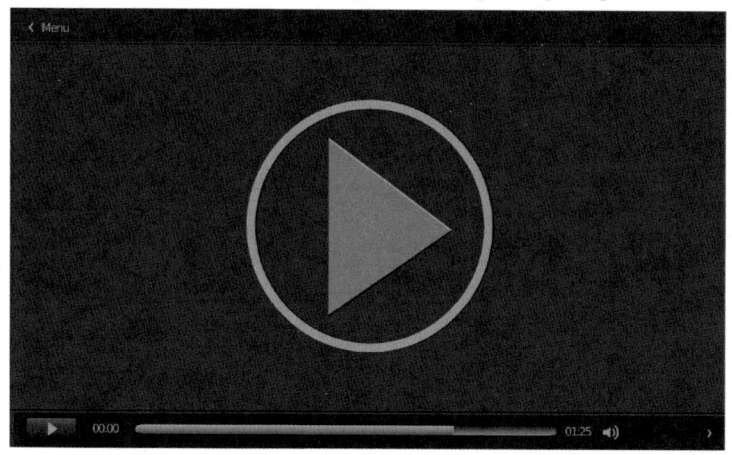

So the girl said can we go home? "mah" said mama "i will like to do more stuff THEN THAT so how about we do not do that", then the girl said an do you have a ps5 an if you do GIVE IT TO MEEEEEE an the fbi will eat the ps5 then they will be a ps5 an now i am a ps5 NOW HERE ME MAMA!!!!!!!!!!!!!!!!

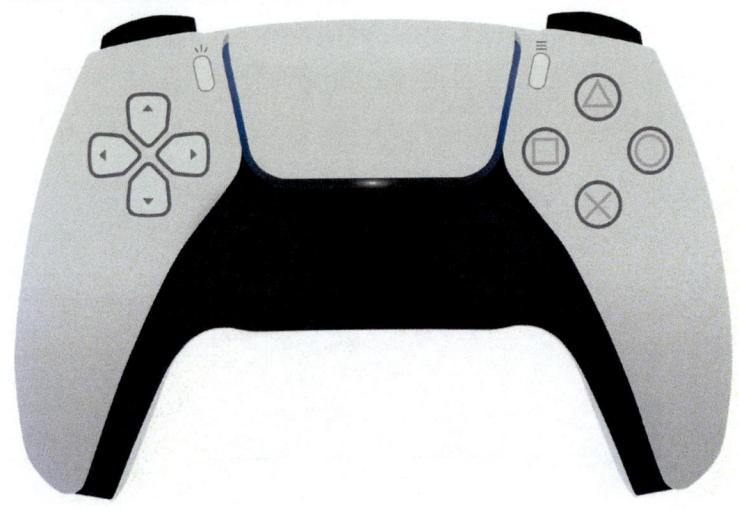

The mother explained that the FBI is a law enforcement agency and they do not give out PS5 video game consoles. What made matters worse was one day, while driving, they almost got into a car accident on the way to school. Then they had to take a new driving route to school. Now they notice that they pass by an FBI building all week long! She shouts out to the building! She screamed out the window: "911!" !! OMG! "NO Stop!", I said, there is no emergency!

And the girl would imagine seeing the fbi in the building. So she would SKREEM HI 911 CAN I GET YOUR AUTOGRAPH MEW

Picasso

The teen also constantly says 911 and talks about 911 frequently. This is very worrying and the mother explained that the helpline for people should not be abused!

What will become of this curious girl only God knows!

Will she become a police officer? This job seems so dangerous in these times, but if it is her passion, she is very brave. She took karate and thinks she is a superhero!

Will she really grow up and join the FBI?

She has practiced arresting her mom! It is surreal!

It is just a total shock and heavy irony for the mother. The father would probably faint if he knew! He was a blackhat hacker, what a shock for us!

Thank you to all first responders and law enforcement for keeping us safe while we write stories about imagining you doing work that we could never do.

I would just like to say in today's age there is a lot of talk about the FBI and politics and well while there can always be some bad apples in the barrel, I like to believe in our law enforcement and have faith that the good solid folks out there fighting crime will remain good.

24

Made in the USA
Columbia, SC
24 April 2023